The Sleeping Party

Springy and Sam

The Sleeping Party

Jan Needle
Illustrated by Robert Bartelt

HEINEMANN · LONDON

For Geraint and Bethan
and, of course, for
Jim and Helena

William Heinemann Ltd
Michelin House
81 Fulham Road
London SW3 6RB

LONDON · MELBOURNE · AUCKLAND

First published in 1988
Text © 1988 Jan Needle
Illustrations © Robert Bartelt 1988
ISBN 0 434 95331 8

Typeset by Wyvern Typesetting Ltd, Bristol
Printed in Great Britain
by Butler and Tanner Ltd, Frome and London

Contents

1 · A Dog Called Disaster

Everybody in The Kerry, when it suited them, agreed that Springy was a nutter.

'It must be the way your mother brought you up,' his father said, cheekily. Then ducked, as Mum hurled a wet dishcloth at his head.

Sam, Springy's sister, said: 'I think the problem is he takes after his father. Don't you, Mum?' And the dishcloth, scooped up off the kitchen floor by Dad, came whooshing across in her direction.

'You're both wrong,' said Mrs Price, ruffling Springy's hair. 'I think young Springy's a one-off. Although he's a twin, there's no one in the whole wide world like him.' A pause and a big grin. 'Thank God!'

Normally, Springy did not like being teased. But today, he didn't care. He was happy. He was full of beans.

'You can laugh,' he said. 'But I give you fair

warning. When Rover wakes up, he'll tear your throats out at my command. He's a vicious killer. Grrrr!'

The family looked at Rover, and Rover did not stir. He was small, ginger – and a cat. As vicious killers went, in fact, he was quite something. That's why Springy was being teased.

'When Rover wakes up,' said Mrs Price, smiling, 'you can start to housetrain him. We've paying guests to worry about, and health regulations and everything. If that cat had come from any other home, it probably wouldn't matter. But Mrs Singleton's . . . well.'

Much as he loved his new pet, Springy had to admit it was a worry. Mrs Singleton was an old woman who had lived alone in a dirty, rundown house full of half-trained animals. She had given him the cat after he and his sister had saved her life. Springy called it Rover because he had always wanted a dog, but had never been allowed.

'What's more,' Dad added, 'we've already had one run-in with one paying guest, and in a way he had a point. So teach the cat to use his litter tray, don't let him near the kitchen, and keep an eye on him. Otherwise – ructions.'

9

'Yeah,' said Sam. 'But that row with Ballantyne wasn't *our* fault, or Rover's. I mean, the man's a –'

She broke off. Ballantyne was a pig, no danger. But she didn't dare to say it. Her mother wagged a finger.

'Get along with you now and do your homework,' she said. 'And Springy – *please* be careful. Whatever you think about Mr Ballantyne, he's here for three months, and his money's important to us. One row's bad enough. We don't want any more.'

Up in their bedroom, Springy and Sam got quite gloomy over it.

'I don't see how we can avoid rows with that pig,' said Sam. 'He's just impossible. I mean *no one*, no one in the whole wide *world*, would have gone on about Rover like he did yesterday. The man's insane.'

Indeed, the problem had been a tiny one. Mr Ballantyne, who sometimes came in late for tea, had found the children still sitting at the table after theirs, cuddling the cat. He had been very nasty.

'Does your mother know you're doing that?' he asked. 'Hasn't she ever heard of the Public Health Act?'

Springy had stood up, blushing. Rover,

sensing fun, had jumped right onto the
tablecloth, among the cups and plates.

'Get him off!' roared Mr Ballantyne. 'That's
disgusting! This is a dining room!'

Mum had heard, and had hurried in from the
kitchen.

'It's only a kitten,' Sam was saying cheekily.
'Are you afraid of it?'

Mr Ballantyne's narrow face had gone even
narrower, and Mrs Price had flashed Sam a dirty
look.

11

'Young lady,' said Mr Ballantyne, 'if I were to call the council . . .'

Their mother interrupted.

'There's no need for that,' she said. 'They shouldn't have it in here. I've told them.'

'But we're only playing, Mum!' said Springy. 'We've finished our tea.'

Mr Ballantyne sneered.

'I suppose you let it in the kitchen as well?' he asked Mrs Price. 'I do think perhaps the authorities should be told.'

Mrs Price went pink.

'Mr Ballantyne,' she said. 'My kitchen is spotless, and the health inspector was here last week. I'll thank you to mind your own business.'

Sam had begun to cheer. But Springy had kicked her under the table. That was the trouble with his sister: no sense of danger.

Over the next few days, although they felt something was bound to go wrong, the children tried their best to wish it away. Sam covered up the little mistakes her brother made if she could, and for Rover the training went on. He was shown his cat litter, and where he should eat, and where he was allowed to sleep, time after time after time. Springy really tried very hard indeed.

12

Sadly, though, Rover was a young cat, and he had come from a bad home. Sometimes he did things right, sometimes he did not. Springy, patiently, followed him about with a plastic shovel, and a brush, and tons of disinfectant. Often, he found him asleep in impossible places – like, for instance, in the grill pan. A disaster just had to happen.

When it did, it could not have been worse . . . Mr Ballantyne, among his other nasty habits, always kept his room locked, although some of the guests did not bother. He made it pretty clear that he did it because he did not trust anybody – even Mrs Bagshaw, The Kerry's cleaning lady.

He did not trust anyone, he said, because of how rough the area was. There had been a few burglaries and break-ins lately, and to Mr

Ballantyne, it just proved how low the people who lived round about must be. As usual, he said it with a sneer.

But although he did not trust Mrs Bagshaw, and did not like her budgie, she had to clean his room. When she was due to, if he was in The Kerry and not at work, he left it unlocked. Only for a few minutes, though! And often, as she hoovered and tidied, he popped back, to check on her, as if she might be stealing something, or looking at his precious papers. When he was not at home, he did not even let her use her master key to get in. The room stayed uncleaned.

The day of the disaster, Mr Ballantyne was downstairs on the phone. No one knew what his business was, but he kept strange hours – sometimes out, sometimes in – and he spent a lot of time on the telephone. While he talked, Mrs Bagshaw did his room. When she had finished, she left it. And by some strange stroke of awful luck, she left the door slightly open. Perhaps the catch was not quite right. It did not click on.

Ten minutes later, the quiet of The Kerry was split by an appalling roar of rage. Mrs Price, and Sam and Springy, dropped what they were doing and raced upstairs. As they reached the first landing Rover, like a streak of ginger lightning, flashed screeching past their legs and downstairs.

15

Springy, horrified, did not know whether to follow or go on.

Mr Ballantyne appeared in his doorway, yelling blue murder. He was red with rage. He could hardly speak.

Mum said: 'Mr Ballantyne. Wha –'

He shouted at her, his eyes bulging.

'That filthy cat! Those children! This *dump*! I'll ... I'll ... I'll ...'

Sam looked at Springy. Springy looked at Sam.

They turned and ran.

2 · What Rover Did

The way Mr Ballantyne went on about the accident, you'd have thought Rover had eaten his gold watch at least. Springy and Sam, hiding in the cellar, listened to the row going on upstairs with their minds boggling.

At first, they could only hear the voice of the Chief Pig. He was shouting so loudly that Sam swore he'd have the windows out. Her brother, though, was too frightened to make jokes of any sort.

Mum's voice was quieter than a man's, unless she was roaring, so they did not expect to hear much in reply. But after a short while they did hear other voices. They were loud as well, and getting louder.

Mr Ballantyne yelled something about the public health inspector, although they could not hear the words exactly. Then another voice bellowed. It was their strange old lodger, Uncle Jock.

'Why don't you shut up about the public health?' he shouted. 'It was a simple accident! It could happen anywhere!'

Mr Ballantyne boomed some more, then they heard a woman's voice. It wasn't Mum's.

'You've got this thing about pets!' it screeched. 'You tried to kill my budgie! You're a monster!'

Then Mum: 'Mrs Bagshaw, please! Don't bring Trannie into this!'

Mr Ballantyne roared, then, loud and clear even through two doors, a floor and the wall the kids were leaning against.

'This is more like a zoo than a guest house!
And you people are like animals! Those
disgusting children are –'

A sort of hoot of anger from Mum cut that off,
then there was the noise of a slamming door. An
old pickle jar on the cellar shelf rattled.

'Crikey,' said Sam. 'I hope there's not a
murder done. They're moving now.'

They were. The noise of the row went quieter,
as the arguing people went along the corridor, or
into another room. Springy still did not speak.
He felt terrible.

'It's a pity Uncle Jock's so little,' said Sam.
'Dad would have killed old Ballantyne for saying
that to Mum. I wonder where . . .'

She broke off. There was a little mew from a corner. More a squeak. Springy jumped up as if he'd been bitten.

'Rover!' he said, joyfully. '*There* you are!'

'That's funny!' said Sam. 'I was just going to say I wonder where the culprit is.'

It was half an hour before the children dared to come up from the cellar, and that was only after they'd heard people searching for them. A head had been poked into the room, but they had hidden themselves behind some carpet rolls. Springy had put Rover up his jumper to keep him quiet. There were several cellars, full of dirty junk, so hiding was not difficult.

When at last they did emerge, and heard the full story, they wished they'd stayed. Mum was alone in the kitchen, and the way she looked at them made them feel really bad. She didn't shout or rant, she just looked cold and angry. That was far worse.

'And where have you two been?' she asked. 'I called all over. Thanks for leaving me to face the music.'

Springy swallowed.

'Sorry, Mum,' he said. 'We were hiding. We were terrified.'

She made a noise. A kind of grunt.

Sam said: 'We were afraid of what might

happen to Rover, Mum. You know how violent that Ballantyne can be. We heard you rowing.'

Mrs Price almost smiled. But it was a grim, thin-lipped smile.

'Yes,' she said. 'The man is vile, I'll grant you. I thought Uncle Jock was going to hit him at one point.'

'Why don't you chuck him out, Mum?' said Sam, excitedly. 'He's a cheeky rat! It's *our* house, The Kerry, not his!'

'Yes,' said Springy. 'The way he goes on, you'd think . . .'

But they had seen Mum's face. They stopped. They knew the answer already.

'The paying guests *pay*,' said Mrs Price. 'We need the money. Without them, we'd have to sell and go.' She paused. 'And they *are* guests. Remember that. You two are in trouble. Serious.'

Sam could have said: 'Why me? It's Springy's cat.' But for once she was completely on his side. Instead she said: 'What exactly did he do? The little cat?'

Again Mum smiled. A small smile.

'He did his business in Mr Ballantyne's room,' she said. 'Well, in his briefcase, to be precise. On all his work papers and his files.'

Springy gulped.

'What, *wee?*' he asked. His mother shook her head.

'No,' she said. 'The other thing. And if either of you laugh, I'll *murder* you. It could cost us plenty. It could cost us three months' rent if Mr Ballantyne goes. And he wants some sort of compensation.'

Apart from one quick flash when they'd seen it in their mind's eye, the children did not feel like laughing. Bad enough to have Ballantyne for three whole months. Even worse – at least for Mum and the family finances – to have him leave. There was a silence.

'So what's he going to do?' said Springy at last. 'What's our punishment? I don't . . . you're not . . . I can keep Rover, can't I? *Please?*'

'I'm going to leave it to your father,' said Mrs Price. 'He should be home tonight, late. You'll have to stew till then. In the meantime, I've let Mr Ballantyne off a week's rent. That's going to cost you in lost pocket money. I'm sorry.'

'What *all* of it?' squeaked Springy, in shock. 'A whole week's rent? I'll get no pocket money for *months*. Years.'

Mrs Price patted his head.

'I'm not sure yet,' she answered. 'No, not all of it. I'll talk it through with Dad. But Mr Ballantyne wanted worse, I can tell you. Terrible.'

'Yeah,' said Sam bitterly. 'I bet *he* wanted you to get rid of the cat.'

'Not just the cat,' said Mrs Price. 'The budgie too. And you two, if it could be arranged! I don't think Mrs Bagshaw and Uncle Jock would have had much chance, either, if it had been left to him! He wants revenge.'

Springy sighed. He had a nasty feeling in his stomach.

'Mum?' he said. 'Dad *won't* make Rover go, will he? He *won't*!'

'He'll be home late on,' said Mum. 'He had a

run down to South Wales, I think. If he's not *too* late, I'll call you down. If you're not asleep.'

'I won't be! You *bet* I won't be.'

But he was. Their father did not get back from dropping his waggon at the yard until gone two next morning. By then even the anxious children, bog-eyed with worry, had dozed off.

3 · A Problem For Sam

The next morning, when they came down, their father was already in the kitchen, tired and grim. He glared at them, rather than said Hallo – and their Mum pulled them to one side to warn them.

'He's had almost no sleep and a row with Ballantyne,' she said. 'He stormed out. So watch your step.'

Sam goggled.

'A row?' she said. 'Has he gone for good?'

'No,' boomed his father. 'He has not. I was tempted to kick him out, but good sense got the better of me. I *almost* had to apologise.'

He was glowering so hard, that Springy's face turned into a picture of worry. Then his father smiled.

'No, you don't have to get rid of your dog,' he said. 'But this is the green card, lad. One more *ounce* of trouble, and he goes. I've told

Ballantyne. He's got the whip hand on you. So remember.'

Springy smiled wildly. Not just because Mr Price had called Rover a dog, either. Although that had suddenly given him a new idea.

'Thanks, Dad,' he said. 'Thanks, thanks, *thanks*. You needn't even give me a birthday present now.'

Mrs Price laughed loudly.

'Hint hint,' she said. 'All right, Springy. We know it's only a couple of weeks. We hadn't forgotten.'

'But I might hold you to what you've just said,' Dad added. 'You've got a big mouth, kid.' He became serious. 'And if there *is* any more trouble with Rover, you *will* get nothing. Except a thick ear, maybe.'

On the way to school, happy as a lark, Springy told Sam his great idea. First of all, though, he swore her not to laugh. She promised she'd try.

The plan was simple, and his sister fell about. The plan was simple and ridiculous!

'But he's *not* a dog,' she said. 'He's a cat, a kitten. You *can't* train him to be a dog.'

Springy bit his lip.

'Not to bite people, or chase postmen,' he said. 'Don't be *stupid*. But to sit when I say so. And to walk to heel. Things like that.'

Sam saw her mates across the road. She waved them over.

'Hey!' she said. 'Heard the latest? My loopy brother's going to train his cat to be a dog!'

Jo and Jenni already knew it was called Rover, and they'd mocked Springy for that. Now they yelped with laughter.

'My Uncle Fred's got a Doberman Pinscher,' said Jo. 'Maybe they could have a fight some time?'

Over the next couple of days, however, Springy worked at his plan, and took advice. From kids he liked and grown-ups he trusted, not stupid giggly girls.

'Yeah,' said Damon, his best friend. 'My Mum says girls have got over-active giggle springs. Anyone'd think they wore tickly knickers or something!'

Damon's Mum often had a sensible word when you needed one. By the end of the week she had told her son, who told his friend, that she'd read somewhere, once, about a man who'd trained a cat to act like a dog.

'It was up North somewhere,' said Damon. 'Up in the Lake District or somewhere. This cat used to go on a lead and everything. And beg for scraps.'

Try as he might to keep the details of the training programme secret from his sister,

Springy couldn't. For a start – although he did not mention it to anyone – he *liked* her. Secondly, it was very hard to train an animal to sit and beg without being spotted.

She caught him at it after about a week, in their bedroom. She opened the door quietly, and stood for two minutes watching, without him noticing.

Rover – not *really* being a dog – did not seem to notice either.

'Sit!' said Springy, for the hundredth time. 'No, not like that. Here. That's right. Now – sit!'

The cat, on all four feet, watched him and tried to lick his hand. Springy gently tried to

push its tail-end down onto the bed. The cat half moved, then stood again.

'Why don't you try –'

It was Sam. Springy jumped a mile, and turned accusingly.

'Hey!' he snapped. 'If you just laugh, I'll . . .'

But Sam was not laughing. She was interested. She came into the room and closed the door.

'Go on,' she said. 'Have another try. Have you had any luck yet? Or is it hopeless?'

Springy looked hard at her to see if she was trying to take the Mick. Then he grinned.

'I made him do it once, ten minutes ago,' he said. 'But he's a bit like Damon. What does Mrs Jackson say at school? A very low concentration span!'

The upshot was that Sam became as interested in the problem of training Rover to be a dog as Springy was. In fact, she roped in Uncle Jock one day, when her brother was out at chess, and asked a special favour.

When Springy got back that night – full of having won his match – she interrupted him.

'Never mind boring old chess!' she said. 'Uncle Jock says he'll help us build a kennel!'

'What?' said Springy. 'You told him! That's not fair!'

'He knew!' said Sam. 'You told him yourself, you fool. What are you wittering on about?'

But Springy was genuinely angry.

'I was out,' he said. 'He's my dog, not yours. You had no rotten right.'

Sam saw red.

'He's a cat, not a dog, stupid! And if it was left to you, he'd *never* learn to sit!'

They were in the front passage, and their voices were getting loud. Suddenly the door to the TV lounge jerked open. Mr Ballantyne was there.

'Keep the row down,' he said, nastily. 'I'm watching. Why don't you go to your beds? It's late.'

Before they could think of anything to do or say, whether rude or polite, he slammed the door on them. They walked towards the breakfast room, subdued.

But before they joined their Mum and Dad, Springy hissed at Sam: 'He's *my* cat, see? You can help if you want to, but don't go behind my back. If you want your own pet, get one for your birthday.'

The idea of a kennel was dropped, of course. Uncle Jock, when Springy spoke to him, said he'd thought Sam was joking.

The other idea, though, the idea of another pet, did not fade away. For the next day or so, hardly mentioning Rover to her brother, and having nothing to do with training him, Sam brooded on it.

She told Jo and Jenni: 'I want something special. It's my birthday soon, and I want something really amazing. Something that will make people sit up and notice.'

Jenni laughed.

'Why not a dog?' she said. 'A real dog. That would chin poor Springy off, wouldn't it?'

Sam smiled, but it was not what she was after.

'I want a python, or something like that,' she said, as Jo and Jenni shrieked in horror. 'Or a chameleon that eats live blowflies. Or some of them fish that eat people to the bone. Piranhas or whatever.'

'Your Mum would never let you,' said Jenni, wisely. 'You have enough trouble with that Ballantyne already.'

'Yeah,' added Jo. 'You might just as well ask for a crocodile or a giraffe.'

They were right. It was a problem.

But one day, quite by luck, the problem solved itself . . .

4 · Nasty Rumours

Although the row between Sam and Springy over training Rover was soon forgotten, Mr Ballantyne kept up the nastiness like nobody's business. He took every opportunity to complain about the cat – even telling them off for letting it in the TV room – and on at least one occasion Springy saw him aim a kick at it. He kept up his war on Mrs Bagshaw and her budgie, as well.

One Saturday morning, Uncle Jock and the cleaning lady joined the children and the pets for a drink, while Mum was shopping. They were all fed up.

'He never lets go,' grumbled Mrs Bagshaw, dipping a chocolate wholemeal into her cup of milky tea. 'You'd think poor little Trannie was a screech owl. I mean – he doesn't make a *lot* of noise, now does he?'

At that moment, the small green budgerigar opened its beak and shrieked like a large green parrot. They laughed.

Springy said: 'He had another go about poor Rover yesterday. The poor little thing only scratched an armchair.'

'Yeah,' went Sam. 'And what did Mum do? She nearly apologised. It makes you sick.'

'Ah,' said Uncle Jock. 'But your Mum and Dad have problems, never forget that. This place must cost a fortune to keep up.'

The children nodded, sadly.

'I know,' said Springy. 'But that doesn't make it any easier. If I was Dad I'd leather him. Honest.'

Sam added: 'I'm having a tiger for my birthday. Or a tarantula. That Ballantyne needs *death*.'

Mrs Bagshaw tutted, and Uncle Jock grinned. But Springy looked at his twin curiously. They could often guess what the other was thinking – and he thought she was up to something. Later, when they were alone, he grabbed her arm.

'What's this about your birthday?' he demanded. 'What have you got up your sleeve?'

'My arm!' she said. 'And you're sticking your fingers in. Let go.'

When he tried to make her tell, the row blew up again. They parted enemies, and for the next few days, Sam went back to brooding. She wanted, she *needed,* something rare and wild and different. But how?

On Tuesday, she chose the worst possible time to bring the subject up with Mrs Price. It was an hour after school, and Sam had made a pot of tea. Everything, in fact, was looking good. Springy was upstairs, and there were just the two of them in the kitchen. When Mum came back from answering the telephone, Sam started.

'Mum,' she said. 'About my birthday. Alton Towers is great, but I want a pet as well. I want a tankful of piranhas.'

She had not looked at Mrs Price's face, because she was busy pouring tea. But the sound of Mrs Price's voice made her snap her head back in shock.

'Oh shut *up*, you stupid, selfish girl!' her mother said. 'Don't you *ever* think of anyone except yourself?'

'Mum,' said Sam, helplessly. She spilt some tea.

'*Now* look!' snapped Mrs Price. 'You are utterly, *completely* useless!'

They stared at each other. Her mother's face was pale, and shocked. To Sam's horror, she looked near to tears.

'What's up?' she said. 'Was it the telephone?'

There was a long pause. Mrs Price tried to get her face in order. When she replied, she still sounded slightly choked, though.

'I'm sorry, love. Yes. Bad news. Another two apprentices have cried off.'

'Crikey,' said Sam. 'But we were counting on them, weren't we? Next week?'

'Of course we were. Of *course* we were. And they're the second, aren't they? In four days. And they said . . . on the telephone . . . they . . .'

The door bounced open, and Springy breezed in, with Rover on his shoulder, on a lead. He was beaming.

'Sam!' he said. 'Mum! I got him to walk to heel. I – oh. What's up?'

Mum's face had got the wobbles again. She began to head for the kitchen door, looking away from them. But as she reached it, it opened yet again. Their father, with grease on his face and wearing a blue boilersuit, smiled in. The smile lasted about a second.

'Jean? What's going off, love?'

She bustled past him, and he turned to follow. Then he stopped. He was holding a yellow cloth bag in his hand. A bag like a pumps bag for PE. It was dangling.

'Listen, you two,' he said quickly. 'I'd better go and see what's up. This looks serious.'

'It is,' said Sam. 'Two more lads aren't coming. Mum says –'

'Heck,' said Dad. 'Look, hang onto this. Be very gentle with it, and don't let it out of your sight. And for God's *sake,* don't open it.'

The children looked at the bag in fascination.

'Why?' said Springy.

'What's *in* it?' added Sam.

Mr Price thrust it into her hand. It wasn't heavy. Just like a pair of pumps. Perhaps it was a pair of pumps.

'I think it might be your birthday present,' he said. 'But *do not open it*.'

Oh, thought Sam. She was really disappointed. It *was* a pair of pumps. Bound to be.

'Dad?' she began. But Dad was gone.

Springy wanted to try and guess what their father had brought home from his travels this time. He also wanted to show off Rover's trick. But his sister was upset.

'We've got to listen,' she said. 'There's something going on, isn't there? Mum said the apprentices *said* something on the phone. She was almost crying.'

Springy felt a twinge in his stomach. He did not like it when Mum cried. Since they'd moved to The Kerry she had done, quite a lot.

'All right,' he said. 'But if they catch us . . .'

They were as quiet as mice, creeping up the stairs. They were as guilty as criminals, lurking on the landing. Rover leapt off Springy's shoulder as they put their ears to the bedroom

door, and ran away. Perhaps he knew they were doing wrong . . .

They could not hear all of it, and a lot of Mum's words were muffled. She was probably crying, they thought, with her head in Dad's shoulder. But some of his replies were clear enough, and they made perfect sense.

'False pretences, Jean?' he said. 'They accused you of telling lies about the place? What the hell's been going on?'

Muffled noises from their mother. They heard the words 'dirty rooms', 'appalling food', 'doss house for tramps'.

Then Dad said: 'Well someone has been putting stories round, haven't they? Telling lies about the place. What did the lads say? "We were well warned off"? Hhm.'

Their mother talked some more. They heard the names of the neighbours across the road. They'd always hated the Prices, because they'd been friends of the people who owned The Kerry before. Mrs Price had said some very hard things about the way they'd left the place when the family moved in.

Father said: 'Well it could be them, I suppose. But then, the students next door are pretty wild. Maybe one of them's got a bee in the bonnet because I tell them off over the noise sometimes.'

44

He did. Occasionally the students had wild parties. Dad, being a lorry driver, needed his sleep. So did paying guests.

Suddenly, Mum's voice came very clear. She'd lifted her face out of her husband's neck.

'Look at the *time*, Jeff! Oh heck, I've got the meals to do!'

Springy and Sam did not wait for any more. They whipped across the landing like greased lightning, and down the stairs. When Dad came into the kitchen a minute later, they were innocently standing. He grinned, as if nothing at all was up.

'That's Mum all right then,' he said. 'Nothing a good night's sleep won't cure. Now – how about a cup of tea?'

They did not mind the lie. In fact, it was necessary, of course. It was meant to make them feel better, or safe at least, and it did. For a while . . .

Then Dad pointed at the bag.

'Glory,' he said. 'Is it still asleep? Haven't you even poked your nose in?'

The kids looked at the bag, still dangling from Sam's hand. Almost as if their father's words had been magic, it began to wriggle and squirm. Like crazy. Sam jumped.

'What *is* it?' she squeaked.

'It's a *snake*!' went Springy.

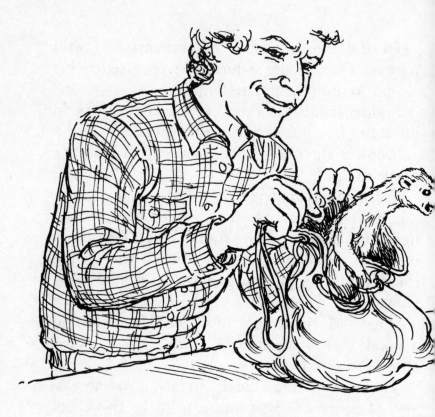

Mr Price hooted with laughter, and took the
bag. He undid the neck-string very carefully,
and eased it open. With amazing quickness, a
head popped out. It was pale yellow, and
pointed, with red, glittering eyes. The mouth
opened pinkly, to show evil little teeth, as sharp
as needles.

'It's a ferret,' he said. 'Some nutter of a lad I
gave a lift to left it in the cab. I told him I didn't
want it, so he sneaked it onto my bunk while I

wasn't looking. I thought you were after a pet?'

How did he know, wondered Springy. Sixth sense. But Sam wasn't wondering anything. She'd gone wild with excitement.

'Oh *Dad!*' she said. 'He's *beautiful*! Can I keep him? Can I touch him? Can I hold him?'

They heard their mother walking down the passageway, but the children hardly noticed. Sam was reaching out to touch the thin, wild head.

Their mother said: 'Jeff, you're mad. As if we haven't got troubles enough.'

'Look out!' shouted Dad. 'Don't touch him, Sam! He'll –'

He did. Like a snake striking. One second Sam's hand was moving gently in, the next her finger was streaming blood. Her brother almost shrieked.

Mrs Price said: 'That's it. That's the finish. Jeff – get rid of it.'

But Sam was gazing at the ferret with shining eyes. She looked a bit ridiculous standing there. She had her finger in her mouth, sucking off the blood.

She was in love . . .

5 · A Trump Card for Ballantyne

Mum meant it when she said the ferret had to go. She was absolutely certain, determined, set, with her mind made up and cast in stone. She said so. The thing that saved him – and Sam, who said she would have died if she lost her little Ferdinand – was Mr Ballantyne. Mr Ballantyne, naturally, did not know this . . .

It was the same evening, and the family had settled down to a period of truce after the hot war. 'Ferdinand must go,' was Mum's last word, and 'Let's at least sleep on it, love,' was Dad's. The kids were keeping their heads down. In fact, they were doing some tidying up when Mr Ballantyne poked his head into the kitchen from the breakfast room – which he was not supposed to do.

'Mrs Price,' he said, in his unpleasant way. 'If dinner ever *is* going to be ready tonight, I'd . . . Hallo? What's that smell?'

Mrs Price went beetroot red. Springy, the little idiot, blurted: 'It's our ferret. He's called Ferdinand. He's . . .'

If the looks of his mother, father and sister could have killed, Springy would have been ready for his coffin on the spot. A wolfish smile played around the lips of the Premier Pig.

'A ferret,' he said. 'How charming. A ferret in the kitchen of a boarding house. How very health and hygiene conscious.'

'Look, Ballantyne,' said Dad. 'He's not here now. He was here for five minutes. When we've finished cooking, we'll clean . . . I mean . . . *Before* we . . .'

He broke off. The children stared at each other, horrified. What had Dad said? They'd clean up the ferret smell when they'd cooked Ballantyne's meal. Oh, blimey . . .

The nasty paying guest gave a sigh of pleasure.

'My, my,' he said. 'I hope you don't intend to let the ferret stay. I hope it's only passing through to a more *suitable* home. I mean – that dirty little cat is bad enough . . .'

Springy and Sam both knew what the other was thinking, and feeling. They both had huge, hollow pits in their stomachs. There was now no doubt. Ferdinand would have to go. Then their mother surprised them both.

'Look, Mr Ballantyne,' she said levelly. 'Quite honestly I'm getting rather sick of your complaints. You may not have realised it yet, but The Kerry is *our* house, and *our* home, and is very little to do with you in any way. You pay to stay here, and you are a guest. If I wanted to, I could get that ferret sent away, and if I wanted to I could give you notice to quit. At the moment, I'm very tempted.'

The children and Dad were tense and silent with shock. So was Ballantyne. He coughed. A nervous cough.

'I was merely remarking, Mrs Price – ' he started. But Mum interrupted.

'You were interfering,' she said. 'If you don't like the house, or the children, or the budgie, or the kitten, or the ferret – go. I can promise you that the Health Regulations will be strictly followed. To the letter. If the authorities are called in, it will be you who looks stupid, not us.'

Now it was Ballantyne's turn to be red. He had lost his sneery smile.

'I've a good mind to leave,' he said. 'It's the last straw. It's like an animal madhouse.'

Mrs Price turned away.

'If you want to go, go,' she said. 'If you want your dinner, sit down. You're not meant to be in my kitchen anyway.'

She walked briskly to the cooker.

'If that ferret causes one ounce of trouble,' she went on, 'or escapes, or frightens anyone, or is allowed to get smelly, or *anything* – it goes. You have my promise. But until that moment, I'll thank you to stop insulting me and my family. I've had enough of it. Now sit down.'

Mr Ballantyne blocked the doorway for a moment longer, as if he meant to argue on. Then he turned, without another word, and went to the breakfast room to wait for his dinner.

Mr Price quietly closed the door. The three of them crowded round Mum and gave a silent cheer. They almost popped their buttons trying

to keep the noise down.

Mum smiled wanly.

'I feel as if I've run a marathon,' she said. 'Jeff – give me a drink. And you two – especially Sam – take note of what I said. One slip, and the ferret goes. Especially a slip over cleanliness. Do you understand?'

They did.

How do you look after a ferret? That was what they needed to know next, and they needed to know quickly. What they did find out was that not many people in a city seemed to know, and books on the subject are hard to find.

Even Uncle Jock, who knew everything about

most things, knew nothing about ferrets. Even
Damon's Mum had not a clue, because Sam and
Springy asked him to ask her. Damon gave them
that bit of bad news during a lesson one
afternoon.

Mrs Jackson, the fiddle-faced teacher with the
crazy sense of humour, rapped her table.

'Listen,' she said. 'I know as teachers go I'm
exceedingly boring, and I know as lessons go this
one has hardly gripped you by the throat. But if
you plan to talk, I'll string all three of you up
from the rafters by your thumbs. Got it?'

'Sorry, Miss,' said Damon, cheerfully. 'Here –
do you know anything about ferrets?'

The class burst out laughing. Sam and

Springy blushed for their friend's stupidity.

But when the noise died down, Mrs Jackson replied: 'Of course I do, little weedy one. I'm a teacher. I know everything.'

The class laughed some more, even louder. Mrs Jackson meant it, though. She had, she told them, had two ferrets when she'd been a girl, and her Uncle George still kept one, called Yellowtooth.

'What I don't know about ferrets,' she said, 'just ain't worth knowing, pardners. For a small fee, I'll tell you everything, after school. Now – back to geography.'

Over the next week or so, with Mrs Jackson's guidance, the children settled Ferdinand in. He had a stout wooden hutch with a double wire top and a quiet box, his bedding was changed every other day, and he tried a variety of foods. The children hoped he would eat cat food, like Rover, but Ferdinand turned up his pretty, dangerous little nose at it. He liked his meat very raw, and very bloody. Liver best of all . . .

Despite Mum's worries, he settled in very well, and very quickly. He learned to recognize the family in days, and stopped biting them on sight. He loved to play, very much like a kitten, and would chase a cotton bobbin for ages. Then, quite suddenly, he would curl up in a ball and go

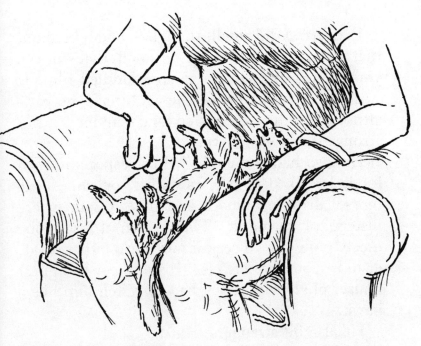

to sleep. Often Mum would have him on her lap, and tickle his belly until he made a high mewing noise and spread all four legs out, stomach to the sky. That trick usually ended in a snooze as well. Mum grew very fond of him.

Oddest of all, as Rover's training to be a dog went on, Ferdinand seemed to want to become a cat. He liked to trot about with little, cat-like steps, he liked to rub himself against people's legs, and he liked to lap milk from a saucer. After a wary start, he and Rover got on very well, and often curled up in one bundle of fur, yellow and ginger, for a sleep.

Ferdinand did smell, though – no doubt about that. It was a sharp, lingering smell, that stuck to your hands and clothes if you cuddled him. It was not unpleasant to the children's noses – although adults were not so fond – and it was not strong. But it was there.

He also had some odd habits, especially with food. He liked to take raw liver, or some little morsel dripping blood, and hide it somewhere instead of eating it. Then when it had gone nicely pongy, he'd seek it out. He'd either eat it, or hide it somewhere else. It was dicey in a guest house, obviously. They had to watch him like a hawk.

He also bit strangers. Hard.

So Mum, much as she liked him, kept up her warnings. One afternoon, when she walked into her empty kitchen and found him on the table, scratching at a parcel of uncooked meat, she went wild with anger.

'Samantha!' she roared. 'Stephen! Come here at once, the pair of you. This awful animal! Oh.'

Ferdinand was terrified by the noise. He did not make a sound, or a movement. He stood up on his hunkers, like a squirrel, with his front paws in front of him as if he was saying a prayer. He froze, a little, yellow statue.

Sam and Springy rushed into the kitchen.

They had been searching everywhere for him.

'Oh Mum!' said Sam. 'You've frightened him. Oh look? Is he going to die?'

Mum forgot her fury. They stared, full of worry, at the rigid little animal on the table.

Behind them, silently, Mr Ballantyne entered the breakfast room and looked through the kitchen door. They did not see him.

After a moment, as they began to stroke the ferret, he crept away. He was smiling . . .

6 . The Lion's Den

Mum was so shocked by making Ferdinand go rigid that she did not punish the children for letting him escape. When he relaxed again, and became a normal happy ferret after about three minutes, they were all silly with relief. Ferdinand got cuddled so hard that he gave Springy a warning nip.

Later that evening, though, when he was asleep in his cage and Rover was ignoring the cardboard indoor kennel Springy had made out of a crisp box, Mrs Price brought the subject up.

'Look,' she said. 'I'm only mentioning Ferdinand because there's some bad news coming up and it's *not* about him. You're going to miss a treat, and it's *not* a punishment. It's a problem.'

They were puzzled. The only treat in the offing was their birthday treat, the following weekend. At the same instant, they both knew.

'Alton Towers,' said Springy. 'We can't go, can we? But Mum, that was the cheapest trip we . . .'

Sam took him by the hand and tried a smile. It didn't work too well.

'Never mind,' she said. 'I've got Ferdie and you've got the dog. What's the trouble, Mum? Cash?'

Mrs Price gave a long, deep sigh.

'What else?' she said. 'I had another cancellation yesterday, and your father and I sat up all night doing the accounts. We're in trouble.'

They were surprised that she did not try to hide it from them. Things must be bad. Springy said: 'Is it the same? Has someone been telling lies about us?'

Mum was startled. She looked hard at them. Then she shrugged.

'I don't know how you know about that,' she said, 'but yes. Someone's been spreading stories. If they don't stop soon, the business will be ruined.'

When Dad came home, they had a family talk. Ideas of new bikes, or Cindy swimming pools, or even Alton Towers, soon became a distant dream. That was one of the troubles with being a twin. All that birthday spending on the same solitary day.

'But what your Mum and I thought,' said Dad, 'is that we'd have special parties for you. It's not much, but it's something. What do you think?'

'Parties?' repeated Sam. 'Did you say part-*ies*? More than one?'

Dad laughed.

'Well – one each. That's fair, isn't it?'

This sounded good. The children perked up.

'On different days?' said Springy. 'Well, they'd have to be, wouldn't they?'

But that was not the idea. The idea was better.

Sam was to have a swimming party in the local baths, with Jenni and Jo and any other friends she wanted, on the Saturday afternoon. Then on the Saturday evening, Springy was to have a sleeping party. His friends could stay all night.

'All *night*,' squeaked Springy. 'Oh, fantastic. How many can I have? Can I have the whole class? Can I –'

Mum wagged a finger.

'It's a boarding house, love. What we thought might work, is if you have Damon and a few pals to the swimming party, then Jenni and Jo join the sleeping party. Plus Damon, of course. That'll be five of you in all. How does that suit?'

If the twins hadn't been good mates, as well as twins, it would have sounded terrible. A big party for Sam, with the boys tagging along, and a small one for Springy – only one friend – with a couple of girls thrown in. But they *were* good mates.

'It sounds *brilliant*,' said Springy. 'Can we have a midnight feast?'

'You can have anything you want,' said Dad. 'As long as you remember: it's a guest house. You can lark about but you mustn't upset anyone. You can be noisy, as long as you stop when you're told. We don't know who'll be staying, but given our bad luck Ballantyne will be here that weekend. And we *need* all the guests we can get . . .'

The excitement on the morning of the party day was terrific. As well as cards, there were small presents at breakfast. There was a model of his father's lorry for Springy, made by Uncle Jock, a wardrobe of dresses for Cindy and Barbie for Sam, made by Mrs Bagshaw, toys and sweets from Mum and Dad. There was also a half-pound of raw liver, gift-wrapped, which Sam had to open messily at table, and a big coloured paper bag for Springy. It was full of dog biscuits.

Everybody laughed. It was a good job Mr Ballantyne had got in very late last night. If he'd looked into the kitchen and seen the animal food on the table, there would have been ructions.

The other excitement was the news Mrs Bagshaw had brought. The spate of break-ins had come very close to home indeed. The tennis club behind The Kerry had been burgled, with the loss of hundreds of pounds from the safe and the fruit machines, and dozens of bottles of whisky and gin. They were all surprised they had heard nothing in the night, but watched with interest as policemen and detectives searched the tennis courts and the nearby bushes.

The swimming party was noisy and great fun, and the birthday tea for Springy and Sam, Damon, Jenni and Jo a riot of giggles, jelly and pop. When Mr Ballantyne poked his surly nose in to make a nasty comment, Mr Price almost shouted at him. Uncle Jock, grinning under his tartan hat, made a rude noise with his mouth.

But it was later, when the adults had left them alone and they were having a breather between noisy, violent games, that a note of real excitement crept in. It was Damon, lying across

Sam's bed and panting, who brought it up.

'That burglary,' he said. 'In the tennis club.
You know who did it, don't you?'

They all looked blank. No, they did not know.

'Well, it stands to reason, don't it?' asked
Damon. 'It was that Ballantyne. You said he was
in late last night didn't you? You said he seemed
to work all crazy hours, sometimes here,
sometimes not here. He's a burglar. It stands to
reason.'

Jenni and Jo laughed at Damon, pointing

mocking fingers. But to Sam and Springy, it was like a blinding flash.

'Shut up, Jo,' said Sam, pushing her friend. 'He might be right. That Ballantyne's a pig. He *does* do funny things. He –'

'He said he was staying for a week,' said Springy. 'Then it was a fortnight, then he said three months!'

'And all that time,' said Sam. 'All those break-ins! It *must* be him!'

Now he'd started it, Damon got nervous. The girls, frankly, thought it was a load of cobblers. The argument went back and forth, and got quite heated. It nearly turned into a shouting match. In the end, they gave it up and went to play with Rover and Ferdinand. Jenni and Damon got bitten, and Jo got scratched by the cat. But in an hour, they were all good friends. So good, in fact, that when hide and seek was suggested, Rover and Ferdinand – whether they wanted to or not – joined in.

The game was fast and furious, and very silent. Despite the hopes of Mum and Dad, there were no other guests in The Kerry that weekend, so the children had lots and lots of rooms to hide in. The rules were simple, and they agreed them among themselves – no getting on or in beds and messing them up, and no making things untidy.

Although they almost killed themselves being quiet, they still managed to upset old Ballantyne. He popped out of his room twice to shout at passing children, and finally stormed downstairs to watch TV, which he turned up very loud. Damon heard him go, and he told the others his door had almost come off its hinges with the bang.

'I went back along the passage after,' he said. 'I think he may have bent the catch or something. He's slammed it so hard it's come open again. The man's cracked.'

'You're cracked,' said Sam. 'He always locks it, div. It won't be open.'

Before there could be an argument, Jo turned up, looking worried. She had been hiding with Ferdinand, and the others were meant to be searching for her.

'What do *you* want?' said Jenni. 'You're it. Go and hide, you fool.'

'I've lost the ferret,' she said. 'He jumped out of my arms. Have you found him yet?'

They had not. They gathered round her, frantic.

'Oh *no*!' said Sam. 'He could go *anywhere*. What floor were you on?'

'The middle one,' said Jo. 'Near the second bathroom. Oh Sam, I'm sorry!'

Two minutes later, they had searched almost every room on the middle floor and they were in the corridor again. There was a gloomy silence, broken only by the booming of the television set downstairs.

'Now you've done it,' said Damon. 'There's only one room left. Ballantyne's.'

As Damon had said, the door was open a crack. Springy and Sam could hardly believe it. The Chief Pig must have been *furious* not to have noticed. But the crack was easily big enough for a ferret to worm through.

Sam's mouth was dry.

'We'll have to look,' she said.

'No!' went Springy. His voice was high and scared.

The two girls said nothing. But Damon giggled.

'I don't know if we'll find Ferdinand,' he said. 'But I do know what we *will* find. Stolen loot!'

'Hey!' said Jenni.

'Yeah!' said Jo.

'Come on!' said Damon.

Sam and Springy were not so sure. They knew Ballantyne. They knew the problems of their Mum and Dad.

But on the other hand . . .

What if the room *was* full of stolen goods . . .?

'There'll be a reward,' said Damon, eagerly.
'Millions!'

His hand was on the door knob.

'And you've *got* to find poor Ferdinand,' said
Jo. 'Haven't you?'

Somehow, they were in.

All five of them in Mr Ballantyne's room.
Damon, the boldest for once, turned on the
light.

7 · The Attack

Sam and Springy, because they lived there, had seen inside the room before. It was just an ordinary guest house room to them, with two narrow beds, a wardrobe and a spindly-legged dressing table. What made it different was that it was *his*. It was forbidden. It was dangerous.

But to the other three, the room was a complete disappointment. Because they did not know how awful Ballantyne was, they were not that scared. It was just a room.

Worst of all, there was no treasure in it. A few clothes across one of the beds, a couple of cases, some books on the dressing table beside a typewriter. No treasure – and no ferret, either.

'Ruddy hell,' said Damon. 'It's boring. Where's all the loot, then?'

Sam said: 'That was a daft idea anyway, wasn't it? Ballantyne a burglar! You're thick.'

She and Springy were all for getting out, while

they had the chance. But Jo and Jenni started clattering about.

'Try the wardrobe!' said Jenni. 'He'll have stuffed it in there! What's gone from the tennis club? Silver cups and stuff?'

Before they could stop her, she had jerked open the wardrobe. She started scrabbling through the suits and jackets hung up inside.

'No!' went Springy. 'Jenni, you'll get us killed! Leave his things alone!'

Jo and Damon, seeing the fun of searching, darted to the dressing table. Damon knocked the books onto the floor as Jo dragged the top drawer open. Sam and Springy had gone white.

'Papers!' said Jo. 'It'll be letters to the chief

crook in London or something. Or pawnshop tickets.'

'Fence, that's the word,' said Damon. 'That's what they call the crooks who buy stolen goods off the burglars!'

'Leave them be!' hissed Sam. 'They're his private letters! He'll remember his door's unlocked and come up!'

Somehow or other they could not make their friends see the danger they were in. Somehow their friends thought it was all a laugh.

'Oh my God,' said Springy to his sister. 'We'll get murdered. Get them *out* of here!'

They were making a noise as well. A lot of noise. Damon, Jenni and Jo did not even notice when the door opened. They did not notice when their friends went rigid with shock and terror, their mouths stuck open.

But when Mr Ballantyne shouted, they nearly leapt out of their skins. It was so loud, it almost deafened them.

'What the hell is going on in here!' he roared. 'Just what are you lot doing! I'll call the police! I'll . . . I'll . . .'

Then he was gasping, unable to speak because he was so filled with rage. The children were like statues, white. Someone was making a very small noise, out of sheer terror.

74

At last they heard footsteps, pounding up the stairs. Dad arrived, then Mum. They crowded into the doorway, beside the paying guest. They both looked horrified.

'Oh!' said Mum, at last. 'How *could* you do this to me? How *could* you?'

The next few minutes were confusion, which luckily involved the grown-ups more than the kids. Mr Ballantyne began to shout at Mum and Dad, and Mum and Dad fought back. One by one, then in a group, the children slipped past them, and got into the passage. They hovered for a moment, than ran. In the bedroom, with its extra mattresses and a table laid out ready for the midnight feast, they huddled together, scared and silent, and listened to the distant row. Nobody spoke for quite a while.

But when the noises from the grown-ups died down, they began to talk again, in whispers. And Jenni said to Jo: 'What've you got there, Jo? Why did you bring them with you?'

Jo looked at her own hands in complete surprise. She hadn't even known she was holding anything. She was, though, and she'd rolled and picked at them until they were all scruffy, and damp with sweat.

It was the bundle of Ballantyne's papers, held together with a Bulldog clip.

Before they could die of fright at what she'd done, the children heard Mr and Mrs Price in the passageway. Sam grabbed the papers and thrust them under her pillow.

'Shut up,' she hissed. 'You've never seen them, right? Oh Jo, you *berk*!'

The parents were grave. They did not rant and rave, but they wanted to know the truth. Damon, to give him his due, did brilliantly.

'It wasn't their fault,' he said bravely. 'We were playing hide and seek, and we lost the ferret. We didn't know it was out of bounds, that room. Me and Jo and Jenni went in, and Sam and Springy tried to stop us. They only came in

to tell us to get out. It wasn't their fault.'

Nice one Damon, thought Springy. He tried to give his pal a grin without being seen by his parents. Too dangerous, though.

Mr and Mrs Price were not all that impressed. They knew the children knew about Ballantyne. All of them. They did not melt.

Mum said: 'Mr Ballantyne is furious. Dead right, too, and you all know it. He's a guest here, and you broke into his room. He wants you punished, and we agree with him.'

Sam said: 'We didn't break in. It was . . .' A look from her father shut her up.

Mum went on: 'It's too late to send you others

home, because your Mums and Dad aren't expecting you. But you're going to bed, now, early, and the lights are going off. The midnight feast is cancelled.'

Springy's lip began to quiver.

'Lights?' he said. 'Are you going to make us go in different rooms? Split us up?'

'No,' said Mum. 'There's no point. We know you'll keep talking for ages anyway. Quite honestly, I can't be bothered shifting mattresses. I'm sick to death of you. But the fun is over. I mean it. Go and use the bathrooms, everyone. Teeth cleaned, faces washed. Me and Mr Price will clear the food away. When you're ready, straight to bed. No lights and no messing. Otherwise there'll be *proper* trouble.'

She did kiss them goodnight, her own children and Jo, who wanted it, and she did listen when Springy and Sam whispered they were sorry. All she said, though, was 'Hmmph.' When Sam worried about poor lost Ferdinand, Dad said he'd find him. He hoped for their sake, he said ominously, that he was not anywhere that Ballantyne could complain about. For fifteen minutes after they had gone, the children all lay quiet, thinking their own sad thoughts. It was a rotten ending to the party.

At last, of course, they began to feel better.

Jenni started it. Her father and mother ran a pub, and she knew the ropes. Her whisper cut the quiet air like a knife.

'I've got two litres of coke in my bag,' she said. 'And eight packets of crisps. I'm *starving*.'

'Ssh,' said Springy. 'You'll get us into trouble.'

There was a babble of 'Oh shut up!' and 'Chicken!' and 'Wimp!' Half a minute later, everyone was milling round in the dark trying to get the feast together.

'A torch,' hissed Damon. 'I've got one in my anorak. Where did I put it?'

Sam had one as well, and both the twins had lots of sweets left from the morning. Soon all five of them were sitting on one bed, ready to start. Springy suddenly jumped off.

'I know!' he said. 'Rover's biscuits! *He'll* never eat them, I bet!'

'They're *dog* biscuits!' said Jo. 'We can't eat them!'

'Why not? I bet they're smashing. They're good shapes, anyway. What do you fancy – a bone or a heart!'

In the light of the two torches, and trying to keep their voices down, they munched dog biscuits (quite good), swilled coke, and made short work of the crisps and sweets. They talked about Ballantyne, and worked out lurid plans to

79

creep down to his room and murder him. It was quite some time before anyone remembered the bundle of papers under the pillow.

Or, for that matter, Ferdinand the ferret.

Jo, picking dog biscuit crumbs from off the front of her pyjamas, said: 'Hey – those letters. Shall we have a look at them?'

'No!' said Springy. 'Leave them be. Perhaps he'll never notice!'

'Oh come on,' said Damon. 'We're in it now. I bet they'll just be boring stuff and we can chuck 'em. He'll think he lost them somewhere.'

The bundle was pulled out. The Bulldog clip was taken off. They fought to get the best position to read them. And very rapidly, they were hooked. Their mouths hung open.

The letters were complaints. They were about dog muck on the pavements, swearing on the telly, the way children behaved on buses – everything. But most of all, they were about The Kerry. They were carbon copies of things that Ballantyne had sent out to people. They were *awful*.

'I can't believe it,' breathed Sam. 'I just cannot believe it. You can't say things like this!'

Just at that moment, there was the most amazing commotion from the floor below. There was a loud roar, halfway between a scream and a

bellow. Then there was shouting, and crashing, and banging. Then they heard running feet, and a woman's scream. Then they heard Uncle Jock pounding down the stairs from the attic room above them.

They looked at each other in the strange light of the torches. They jumped off the bed. They rushed for the light switch, and the door. They jerked it open.

From the stairwell came the cries of a man in pain.

'I've been attacked!' the voice yelled. 'I'm bleeding! Call an ambulance!'

It was Mr Ballantyne . . .

8 · Pink Pig

Mr Ballantyne, it turned out, had done them a service. He had found the missing ferret. Ferdinand, fed up with hide and seek, had gone to bed. He had sneaked into the Chief Pig's room, slipped in beside the Chief Pig's pillow, and wormed his way down under the Chief Pig's duvet.

While the children had searched the room earlier, Ferdinand had lain low. He'd probably been asleep.

But when Mr Ballantyne had got into his striped pyjamas, happy in the knowledge that he'd wrecked the children's sleeping party, Ferdinand had woken up.

What was this alien foot poking into his new den? What was this skinny, hairy leg poking out of a stripy pair of trousers? Who was this large person, grunting and pushing?

Ferdinand had selected the softest and whitest

piece of exposed flesh – and sunk his fangs in. When Ballantyne ran down the passage, the ferret was still hanging on for dear life, his pointed little teeth almost meeting in the middle of his bite. He had only let go when Dad had run along to find out what the row was about. The ferret had jumped to the carpet and come up to him for a cuddle.

A big mistake for the ferret. Because Mr Ballantyne, seeing it in front of him, had given it an enormous kick, that sent it flying down the corridor.

That had been a big mistake for the paying
guest. Because Dad was only stopped from
kicking *him* by the arrival of Mum and Uncle
Jock. There was very nearly a fight.

When the children turned up, it was mayhem.

'Call the police!' Mr Ballantyne was
screeching. 'I demand to see a doctor! My
blood's been poisoned! I'll have this place closed
down!'

'If you don't stop frightening my kids, I'll
close *you* down!' bellowed Dad. 'I'll hit you so
hard you'll see stars for a week!'

'Oh Jeff!' said Mum.

'Go it, Dad!' shouted Sam. 'Bash him one for me!'

'Calm down, calm down,' said Uncle Jock. He looked very funny, wearing only a long tartan shirt and pair of flipflops. Nobody laughed.

'This place is like an insane asylum,' went on Mr Ballantyne. 'It's a cross between a zoo and a playschool. Has that animal had its jabs? I'll get rabies! I'll get rabies!'

Sam shouted: 'You deserve to! You're a nasty, mithering, pig!'

'Shut up, Sam!' yelled Mum. 'Go to bed, the lot of you!'

'Where's the poor little ferret?' wailed Jenni. 'What's he *done* to him?'

'Ferdinand,' went Damon. 'Come on, Ferdie! Here, boy! Here, boy!'

It could not go on for ever, naturally. Even Mr Ballantyne could see it was starting to get ridiculous. He decided to try a new approach. He leaned against the wall, looking as if he was about to faint. He pointed to his foot.

'The blood,' he croaked. 'Call an ambulance, quickly. I'm going to bleed to death.'

Everyone looked, interested. Indeed, blood had run right down his ankle and off his foot. His pyjama leg was soaked in it.

86

'Ooh,' said Sam. 'You'll stain the carpet.'

Mr Ballantyne gave a stagger. It seemed as if he really was about to fall. Everyone went quiet.

'You might think this is all a joke,' he said. His voice was quiet now. But full of menace. 'But you'll laugh on the other side of your faces soon. I'll close you down for this.'

The excitement drained away. They realised he was probably right. Dad went and took him by the arm, and started helping him towards his room. Mum looked at the children, pale-faced and almost tearful.

'Get to bed,' she said. 'Now. Please. No arguments.'

'But what about the ferret?' asked Sam. 'He may be . . .'

Uncle Jock put in: 'I'll find Ferdinand. He'll be all right. He's probably in his cage by now. So get to bed, like Mrs Price says.'

They all turned. Jo had a wobbly lip.

'Come on,' she said. 'I'm sorry, Mrs Price. Oh crikey.'

In the bedroom, they huddled round. There was still a little coke, but no one wanted it. They did not even notice for a moment that Springy was not there. Then, as Damon wondered aloud where he'd gone – he turned up. He looked almost happy.

'We've found Ferdinand,' he said. 'He was on the kitchen table. Uncle Jock's put him away.'

Jenni said: 'Well, that's one good thing.'

Sam replied: 'Oh yeah? D'you think I'll be allowed to keep him after this? *No* chance.'

'Oh no!' said everyone. 'You don't think . . .?'

Everyone but Springy. He was smiling. His sister snapped at him, viciously: 'I suppose you're happy because your stupid cat's not involved, you divot? You're horrible. I hate you.'

Springy said mildly: 'Well I did help find Ferdie, didn't I?'

'Yeah!' she said, nastily. 'And what were you doing downstairs anyway? Creeping to Mum, I s'pose?'

'No,' said Springy. 'I gave her the letters, didn't I? I thought she ought to see them.'

That shut them up. It shut them up completely. They stared at Springy, wondering, for some time. They couldn't make their minds up if it was a good thing to have done or not. For ages, nobody said a word.

'But we pinched them,' said Jo, at last. 'We should never have took them in the first place.'

'Yeah,' said Damon. 'But they're full of garbage, ain't they? Old Ballantyne should never have writ them.'

They remembered the letters, and discussed them. One, half written, was addressed to the telephone engineering college, who sent lots of apprentices to stay at The Kerry. It mentioned dirt, and animals running loose among the foodstuffs on the table, and uncleaned lavatories. Another one, they recalled, had said there was a tramp who hung around the place.

'Blimey!' said Sam, realising. 'That must mean Uncle Jock! The cheeky, cheeky swine!'

They remembered snippets from other letters. About noise, and rude children, and father standing in the kitchen in greasy overalls from work. The letters had gone to the Health people, the city council, all sorts of places.

It gradually dawned on them just what the paying guest had done.

'It was *him*,' said Sam. 'All the time. He was the one putting people off. He's the one who's caused all those bookings to change their minds and cancel. He's nearly made Mum bankrupt.'

'Yeah,' said Damon. 'And to think we thought he was a burglar. This is much worse when you think about it.'

'Not one sort of crook, but another sort,' said Jenni.

'So it must be right to have shown your Mum,' added Jo. 'I think it was brilliant, Springy.'

Springy smiled. He felt all smug.

'Yeah,' he said. 'We thought he was a criminal,

but he was just a nut. We've rumbled him.'

'Ooh, listen to Cleverclogs,' said Sam. 'You're such a bighead.'

'And anyway,' said Damon. 'It was me that went into his room. Me and the girls. You two said we shouldn't. You two said we'd get hung, or something. You two were yellow.'

To be quite honest, none of them was really certain if they'd done right or wrong. They did not know if the morning would bring praise or blame, punishment or reward. They chewed some dog biscuits for a while, and passed the coke round sitting in their own sleeping bags at last. The midnight feast was over. They fell asleep.

Breakfast was late. Breakfast was *very* late. They all sat round the table bleary-eyed. They noticed that Rover had already been fed, and they could hear Uncle Jock humming in the cellar. He'd be feeding Ferdinand, too.

Mum, who had told them to sit in the breakfast room, not the kitchen, had said nothing more. There had been no sign of Dad.

They whispered a little, but not much. They were terrified.

'Mum,' called Springy, once.

'Shut up,' came the reply.

At last, they were all convinced. It was a disaster. This was like the last meal a prisoner got before being hanged. They were in the breakfast room to make them feel posh before the execution.

Then they heard whispering in the kitchen. Dad's voice. He must have sneaked in through the back door.

Then the sound of a trumpet fanfare, made on a pair of lips. One of Uncle Jock's more stupid tricks!

Then Dad appeared, in a funny hat. He was beaming. He was carrying a big bottle of pop and

a *gigantic* plate of cream cakes. Cream cakes for breakfast! Uncle Jock appeared, still blowing his raspberry-trumpet.

'Pray silence for the guest of honour!' said Dad. 'The biggest pig in Manchester! I give you – Mister Ballantyne!'

As the children gaped, Mum stepped into the doorway. On a huge meat plate, she was carrying an amazing cake. It was made of sponge, and pink icing sugar, and ice cream, with Smarty eyes and a curly liquorice tail.

It was a pink pig. A lovely, smiling, eatable – pig.

93

'It's for you,' she said. 'All of you. This is a proper party, to make up for last night.'

Dad said, grinning all over his face: 'Sadly, the real Chief Pig can't be here. He had some trouble over some letters. He had to leave.'

They gasped.

'Gone?!' squeaked Springy. 'When?'

The grown-ups looked at each other.

'Oh,' said Mum. 'It would have been six o'clock, I think. Something like that. Now – hats on, everyone.'

Springy, who was a cautious boy, asked carefully: 'But if he's gone, can we . . . I mean, we need his money, don't we?'

Dad smiled, seriously.

'If you think about it,' he said, 'Ballantyne was costing us a lot more in lost guests than he paid in rent, wasn't he? It'll probably take us a fair old time and a fair number of letters to get back our good name. But if he'd stayed . . . well, who knows what might have happened?'

Mum said: 'We thought of calling in the police, but there didn't seem a lot of point. He seemed to get a kick out of writing nasty letters, not just about The Kerry. Maybe he was sick.'

'Anyway,' Dad added. 'It's not your worry. But I promise you – we'll be all right now he's gone. I promise you.'

94

That was good enough for Springy. And for
Sam. Mum laughed at the relief on their faces.

'Come on,' she cried. 'Five knives! You can all
stick one into him at once.'

They did. It was a fantastic feeling. It was
wonderful.

'He won't be back again,' said Mum.

She paused.

'Thanks,' she said.